' "I hear, Sir Richard, that you have a forest famous for its huge number of animals. Hunting is my passion and the forests in the realm have become sadly depleted."

Sir Richard, Roland, Rosalind and Rosamund all froze mid-mouthful.

"Is something wrong, Sir Richard?" asked the King.

"Eh, no, Your Majesty, but I had, eh, hoped that, eh, you would want to spend tomorrow looking at all the improvements I have made to my estates."

"That's dry stuff, man. No, I want to be up at the crack of dawn and away on the chase. That's my idea of a good day's sport." '

Sir Richard, the Green Knight, has banned all hunting in the forest. But now King Pippin has come to stay and wants a royal hunt! What can be done to save the animals? Perhaps Rosie the Dragon can help . . .

Rosie and the Royal Hunt is the second story to be published by Young Corgi Books about Roland the Minstrel, the Green Knight and Rosie the Dragon.

ROSIE
AND THE
ROYAL HUNT
ANN JUNGMAN

Illustrated by Ann Jasper

YOUNG CORGI BOOKS

ROSIE AND THE ROYAL HUNT
A YOUNG CORGI BOOK 0 552 52702 5

First published in Great Britain by Young Corgi Books

PRINTING HISTORY
Young Corgi edition published 1992
Reprinted 1992

This book is set in 18/24pt Garamond by
Chippendale Type Ltd., Otley, West Yorkshire

Young Corgi Books are published by Transworld Publishers Ltd.
61–63 Uxbridge Road, Ealing, London W5 5SA, in Australia by
Transworld Publishers (Australia) Pty. Ltd., 15–23 Helles Avenu
Moorebank, NSW 2170, and in New Zealand by Transworld
Publishers (N.Z.) Ltd., 3 William Pickering Drive, Albany, Auck

Printed and bound in Great Britain by
Cox & Wyman Ltd., Reading, Berks.

*To Barbara Chamberlain,
with much love*

CHAPTER ONE

THE UNICORN

ello there,' called
Sir Richard as he stood outside
the cave of Rosie the Dragon,
'Anyone at home?'

'Oh Sir Richard love,' came a
voice from the back of the cave,
'I'm in the bath, but I'll be out

7

in a minute. You put the kettle on for a cup of tea and then we can have a nice little chat.'

After a few minutes Rosie came out with a towel round her head and sat down with her guest.

'Well, this is a nice surprise, I must say,' said the dragon, sipping her tea, 'I hardly ever see you these days.'

'Nothing personal, Rosie old girl. It's just that I'm working so hard planting trees and trying out new kinds of crops.'

'Oh, I know all about that, Sir Richard. I've seen you when I go into the village to do my bit of shopping. You look as though you're enjoying it all.'

'I do, Rosie, it's very satisfying planting things and seeing them grow. I always did find it far more interesting than jousting and fighting and all the things knights are supposed to do – as you well know.'

'Yes, well, all the animals in the forest were very relieved when you gave up hunting. They asked me to say thank you for them.'

'Well, that's what I came to see you about, Rosie. I think that I will put notices up all round the outskirts of the forest saying, NO HUNTING PER-MITTED. TRESPASSERS WILL BE PUNISHED. Just to make sure that no-one else uses this forest for hunting purposes.'

'Oh that would be very nice, Sir Richard dear. We'd all

appreciate it so very much. When the word gets around I expect lots more animals will want to come and live here and that would be very nice. The more the merrier, I always say.'

'Yes, turn it into a kind of jolly old animal sanctuary, that kind of thing.'

'That's grand, Sir Richard dear, really grand. You put your notices up and then, well, we'll just have to wait and see which animals turn up.'

The notices banning hunting
had only been up a few days
when deer and stags and foxes
began to trickle into the forest.
Rosie always welcomed them
enthusiastically and showed

them round. One night Rosie was asleep in her cave, when she heard the sound of twigs cracking outside.

'Someone is out there,' she thought to herself and quietly she uncurled and crept to the side of the opening of the cave.

'There definitely is something out there,' she muttered and let out a burst of flame. Something white flickered in the light and let out a high-pitched scream.

'Don't hurt me, Mr Dragon!'

it cried. 'I don't mean any harm. I just wanted to live in the forest where there is no hunting.'

'Well, come into my cave then, whoever you are,' grumbled Rosie. 'And if you start any funny business, I'll turn you into a crispy noodle with just one little burst of my flames.'

'I won't try any funny business,' it whimpered. 'I promise Mr Dragon, please, please don't turn me into a crispy noodle.'

'All right I won't,' agreed Rosie, 'but come on in, I'm catching my death of cold standing out here.'

The white animal quietly slipped out of the shadows.

'Well, bless my soul!' said Rosie. 'If it isn't a unicorn! What a surprise! I never saw a unicorn before. What a beautiful creature you are. Come on in love, welcome to the forest.

Oh, Sir Richard will be so excited when he sees you, to say nothing of the Ladies Rosalind and Rosamund.'

'Who are they?' asked the unicorn suspiciously.

'Sir Richard is the Lord of the Manor and Lady Rosamund is his wife and Rosalind is his daughter and she's married to a minstrel called Roland.'

'I see,' nodded the unicorn. 'And was it they who put up the NO HUNTING notice?'

'Aye, it was that,' Rosie told her. 'You're safe here, not a single thing to worry your pretty little head about.'

'Thank you so much, Mr Dragon, for not turning me into a crispy noodle.'

'Oh, I wouldn't have done it love. I may look fierce but the truth is I wouldn't harm a soul.'

'I'm very relieved to hear that, Mr Dragon.'

'Oh, stop this Mr Dragon nonsense. If it was anything

like that, it would be Miss Dragon but everyone knows me as Rosie.'

'Oh, so sorry Mr, I mean Miss, I mean Rosie. And I'm very glad I found my way to your cosy cave. I think I'm going to really like it here.'

'I'm very glad to hear that love, now let's get some sleep and in the morning I'll tell you all about our very special forest.'

And Rosie and the unicorn curled up at opposite sides of

the cave and slept until the
birds woke them at dawn.

CHAPTER TWO

THE KING

One fine sunny after-noon Sir Richard was helping the farmers plant a row of trees. The ladies Rosamund and Rosalind were picking some blackberries for supper and Roland was digging a hole for a particularly big tree. Suddenly they noticed a horseman riding towards them.

'Whoever can it be?' wondered Roland.

'I think he's wearing the King's colours,' said Rosamund.

'Dash it, you're right!' cried her father. 'It must be the King's herald. I wonder what he wants.'

A moment later the herald stopped in front of them.

'In the King's name, which one of you is Sir Richard de la Rose?'

Sir Richard stepped forward. 'It is I.'

'A Royal Proclamation from His Royal Highness King Pippin the Fourth. Could you read it now Sir Richard, so that I may give your reply to the King?'

Sir Richard unrolled the scroll and read:

'*His Majesty King Pippin the Fourth wishes to inform his subject Sir Richard de la Rose that he is making a royal progress and expects his loyal knight to entertain him and his royal entourage while staying in that part of his realm. Pippin Rex.*'

'What's a royal progress?' asked Roland.

'It means the King and his court are coming to our castle

and we will have to entertain them, for as long as they want to stay.'

'I'll sing for them!' cried the minstrel.

'No you won't,' shouted everyone else.

'Pray tell His Majesty that I will be honoured to entertain him and his entourage,' Sir Richard told the herald. 'When may we expect them?'

'In a week's time,' the herald told him and wheeling his

horse around he rode off in a cloud of dust, calling, 'I'll tell His Majesty that you will be expecting him.'

For the next few days all the farmers and their wives left the fields and helped clean the castle from top to bottom. Sweet-smelling flowers were put in every room, all the silver candlesticks were polished, the kitchen shone like a mirror and clean rush mats were put down on the floors. The day the King was due to arrive, food of every kind was carried into the kitchen under the watchful eye of the Lady Rosamund. Lady Rosalind was already wearing her apron and was busy slicing onions. By the end of the day, the table in the kitchen was groaning under the weight of pies – meat pies and vegetable pies, cherry pies and apple pies, game pies and lemon pies. On the spit meat was roasting and Cook and the ladies Rosalind

and Rosamund competed to see who could make the most delicious sauces.

As evening fell Sir Richard came down into the kitchen in his best robes.

'Oh, what a spread!' he cried. 'How hard you have all worked. My congratulations! And just about everything produced from our own estates! The King will be impressed. Now, off you go everyone and get dressed in all your finery. Come on wife, if the King sees you in an apron with flour in your hair, we'll never live it down. And Rosamund, go and wash and then put your hair up and put some shoes on. The

King could be here any minute.'

Half an hour later a trumpet sounded.

'They're coming,' yelled Cook. 'The trumpet is the signal! Go on everyone, quickly into your places.'

All Sir Richard's tenants stood outside the castle gates waving flowers and cheering as the King rode by. Sir Richard stood on the drawbridge with Roland. Just as the King was dismounting, Rosalind and

Rosamund ran out and curtsied low. Roland and Sir Richard knelt down. The King leapt out of his saddle.

'Sir Richard, rise. What a splendid castle and the land around is well kept, very well kept. This pleases us and your tenants look healthy and well fed. Would that more of my realm was like this.'

'Your Majesty is too kind. May I introduce my wife, the Lady Rosalind, my daughter, the Lady Rosamund and my son-in-law, Roland.'

'Ah, Sir Richard, so not only do you have rich lands but beautiful women also. I warrant me you two ladies have spent all day in front of your mirrors preparing yourselves to greet me, you look so fair and so flushed.'

Rosamund laughed and replied.

'Oh no, Your Majesty, Mother and I . . . '

Sir Richard glared at her and

interrupted hastily, 'Your Majesty, may we show you and your knights to your quarters? We have prepared a banquet fit for a king.'

'Good, good,' smiled the King. 'We have ridden far and are hungry. We will eat in an hour.'

At the banquet the King and his knights sat with Sir Richard's family above the salt and the tenants sat below it. The King ate and ate.

'Lady Rosalind, you must

have a most excellent cook. I
never ate better food. Is there a
bit more of that most excellent
cherry pie? It is my fifth slice
but I cannot resist. Eat up, my

knights, for tomorrow we will hunt. I hear, Sir Richard, that you have a forest famous for its huge number of animals. Hunting is my passion and the forests in the realm have become sadly depleted.'

Sir Richard, Roland, Rosalind and Rosamund all froze mid-mouthful.

'Is something wrong, Sir Richard?' asked the King.

'Eh, no, your Majesty, but I had, eh, hoped that, eh, you

would want to spend tomorrow looking at all the improvements I have made to my estates.'

'That's dry stuff, man. No, I want to be up at the crack of dawn and away on the chase. That's my idea of a good day's sport.'

Roland leapt up and grabbed his lute and began to sing loudly:

'Fal, la, la, la, la, la, la,
  diddle, diddle,

With a hey, and ho and
nonnie, nonnie, niddle,
I will away unto the forest
deep,
And there I will find a
dragon asleep.
I will tell of what is planned
And I'm sure she will have
an idea in hand.
Tra, la, liddle, liddle, dum,
dum, dum.'

'Stop,' cried the King. 'I never heard such a terrible noise.

Come, Sir Richard, let us lead the ladies in a dance. Anything but that terrible singing. He may be your son-in-law but that minstrel can't sing. Musicians, strike up the music. Let the dancing commence.'

As the music began and the dancing got going, Roland slipped out the back door, catching Lady Rosamund's eye as she smiled sweetly at the King.

CHAPTER THREE
ROSIE'S PLAN

Neither the King nor any of his knights noticed Roland's hasty departure, so busy were they enjoying the pleasures of the dance. Once out of the castle, Roland ran as fast as his legs would carry him to the forest. As he arrived at the edge of the forest Roland realized that he had not thought to bring any kind of light with him.

'Oh dear,' he said to himself, 'I won't be able to see a thing and I'll get lost. Oh well, this is an emergency and I shall have to think of something. I know, maybe if I sit by the side of the road here and sing, Rosie will hear me and then she can lead me to her cave.'

So Roland sat down and began to sing at the top of his voice. After a while he was surrounded by large groups of animals all looking puzzled.

'Go and get Rosie,' said the

chief stag. 'I can't stand this terrible noise much longer. The poor man must be in pain. Rosie can talk to people – we need her here.'

'I'll have her here in two minutes, just you see,' grinned a fox and he dashed off into the forest. The animals stood with their hands over their ears and stared at Roland.

'I've heard humans before,' said the unicorn, 'but I never heard one who sounded like that.'

'Poor chap,' agreed the stag, 'but as he's Rosie's friend and the son-in-law of Sir Richard, our benefactor, he must be all right – when he's not ill, that is.'

A moment later Rosie appeared on the scene.

'Oh, Roland love, it's you. Oh, what a relief. The fox told me there was a human person in terrible pain, but it's only you doing a bit of singing. Now what's it all about? Why are you making all this noise at the edge of the forest at this time of night?'

'To attract your attention, Rosie. I sneaked out of the castle because something terrible is going to happen and I had to warn you immediately.'

'Well, out with it. What is going to happen?'

'The King is staying with Sir Richard and he and all his knights are planning to go hunting tomorrow. I rushed out to warn you and all the animals.'

'Oh dear, oh dear,' sighed Rosie, 'I shall have to put a stop to this hunting nonsense once and for all. Come on back to the cave, Roland, and we'll work something out. I've got a naughty little idea that's just beginning to develop very nicely.'

Rosie then told the animals in their own language why Roland was there and was asked to thank him on their behalf.

'I want you all to wait for me outside my cave with your families,' the dragon told them. 'I have a plan and you have to be ready to move as soon as Roland and I have worked out the details.'

Inside the cave Rosie gave Roland a cup of tea and then gave him a pad and a quill pen.

'Now Roland love, I want you to write down the names of all the people in the village who are supporters of Sir Richard.'

'That's just about everyone, Rosie. I mean he's the best Lord of the Manor in the world, everyone knows that. Even the King commented on how well and healthy and contented all the tenants looked. You can rely on one hundred per cent support in the village.'

'Good,' smiled Rosie. 'Then get writing.'

'You can rest the pad on me,' said the unicorn. 'That will make the writing much easier.'

''Thank you,' said Roland

smiling. 'You're not just a pretty face, are you, unicorn?'

'Certainly not,' agreed the unicorn, as Roland completed his list.

'Now,' said Rosie. 'What I want you to do is take one family of animals to each household on this list and ask them to hide the creatures, until I've had time to sort this King fellow out.'

'Sort the King out!' cried Roland. 'Rosie, what exactly are you going to do?'

'You'll see soon enough, love. Now, I'm going to talk to the animals for a minute and then you must take them to the villagers and explain why they must be hidden. Tell the people it won't be for long, twelve hours at the most.'

By the time the sun rose and the King and his knights were ready to leave for a good day's hunting, every large animal in the forest was safely hidden in a villager's cottage. Exhausted,

Roland staggered back to the castle, wondering what on earth Rosie's plan could be.

CHAPTER FOUR

THE ROYAL HUNT

ir Richard and the ladies Rosalind and Rosamund stood on the drawbridge and waved to the knights as they rode off towards the forest. As soon as the hunting party was out of sight they all raced down to the kitchen as fast as their legs would carry them. Roland sat at the big table wolfing down a big bowl of milk.

'What happened?' demanded Rosalind.

'Did you manage to find Rosie all right?' asked Sir Richard.

'What exactly is going on in the forest?' questioned Rosamund.

'I'm not really sure what's happening,' Roland told them.

'Rosie has a plan but she won't say what it is. She says she's going to put a stop to hunting in the forest once and for all.'

'Oh dear,' groaned Sir Richard. 'She is such a headstrong old girl, that dragon, I do hope she doesn't get into trouble.'

'What about the animals?' asked Rosalind.

'Oh, they're fine, I lodged them all out with the villagers. Only the unicorn stayed behind and she's safely hidden at the back of Rosie's cave. The King won't find a thing to kill in the forest today.'

Rosamund giggled. 'He will get a shock, won't he?'

Meanwhile, back in the

forest, the King and his knights rode along the path between the tall trees. The dogs were barking and the knights were all looking around very hard for animals to chase.

'It's most odd,' said King Pippin. 'I had heard that there were more animals in this forest than in any other in the kingdom' 'The biggest thing I've seen is a rabbit,' complained a knight, 'and what's more, I got the feeling that the rabbit was laughing at me.'

The knights all roared with laughter at this comment and continued on their way, getting more and more puzzled. They were almost in the middle of the forest when suddenly they heard a huge roar and then out of a clearing a dragon raced towards them. The dragon was a mass of flames and smoke and deafening roars. The knights turned tail and charged out of the forest as fast as they could. The King made to follow them but the dragon let out a tiny little flame near the royal horse. The King fell off and lay on the grass and watched his horse gallop after the other knights. Standing up, the King drew his sword and prepared to fight the fierce dragon. Much to his surprise, however, the dragon had disappeared.

The King wandered around for a while and then he began

to notice noises he hadn't heard before. They were the sounds of large animals walking through the undergrowth. King Pippin began to have the feeling that he was being followed. It wasn't a good feeling. Not quite knowing why, he began to run. He ran and ran, falling over roots and scratching himself on thorns. When he was completely exhausted, the King stopped. He listened hard. The animals were still following him.

'I just don't understand it,' he muttered to himself. 'None of the animals that live in this forest is man—eating. Why are they hunting me?' Just then he realized that the animals were making a circle round him.

'They're going to close in on me,' he thought, 'I must climb a tree and wait until my knights come to find me.'

After the King had been sitting miserably in the tree for about an hour, he looked down and saw a friendly looking dragon under the tree.

'Good afternoon, Your Majesty,' said the dragon. 'I've just made a nice pot of tea. Would you like to come and drink a cup in my cave?'

'Oh!' said the King, feeling very surprised. 'Well, that is a kind invitation, and you seem like a nice, friendly, civilized kind of dragon (not like some I've met today). But what about the animals? They are all hunting me.'

'Don't worry about them, Kingy dear, they've all gone off home. Now down you come before you catch your death of cold.'

The King climbed down from the tree.

'Kind dragon, I must thank you for rescuing your monarch.'

'It was a pleasure, Kingy dear, now, on my back. Come on, don't waste time, you need a hot drink in front of a nice fire, and no mistake.'

So the King hopped up on Rosie's back and they trotted off through the forest to her cave.

CHAPTER FIVE

CRISPY NOODLE

As soon as Rosie got back to her cave she made a big pot of tea and some toast.

'There you are, Kingy dear, a nice hot cup of tea and some toast. Just what you need to warm you up.'

As he gulped it down, the King burst into tears. Rosie put her arms around him and patted his head.

'There, there, Kingy dear, it's all over, don't you take on like that.'

'Those animals, they were hunting me. It was horrible!'

'Well, there, now you know what it's like. Not very nice, is it?'

The king shook his head.

'That's what we wanted you to realize.'

'I don't understand.'

'Well, it's like this, Kingy dear. Our lovely Sir Richard has forbidden hunting in this forest, so of course a lot of animals have come to live here, for safety, you understand.'

'Eh, well yes, but there didn't seem to be many around when my knights and I were hunting.'

'That's because they were all lodging out with the villagers.'

'Lodging out! In the villagers' houses?'

' 'Course,' replied Rosie. 'You see, when Roland heard that you were all coming hunting in the forest, he came and told me. Well, forewarned is forearmed, and I arranged for my friends the stags and the foxes and the wild boar to be boarded out till this little crisis blew over.'

'So you're behind all of this?'

'Yes,' said Rosie smiling smugly.

'Aren't the villagers frightened of you?'

'Bless you, no. They all know Rosie. I knit sweaters for their children, you see. Sir Richard, bless him, likes us to get together and co-operate. Now, where was I? Oh yes. All the animals left the forest last night, then you and that crew of yours came crashing in. I waited till you were right in the middle of the forest and then I came at you pretending to be really fierce.'

'I remember,' said the King shuddering.

'Good! Serves you right. So you see then, all the brave knights fled and I singed your horse a bit, so that he would throw you. I planned it all,' the dragon told him proudly.

'High treason,' muttered King Pippin. 'What was the next step of your fiendish plan?'

'Well, I told the villagers that as soon as all the knights came charging out of the forest, to set the animals free. Then I told the animals to pretend to hunt you.'

'Why hunt me?'

'So you would get to know what being hunted is like. Then, I decided, once you realized how cruel it was, you would ban hunting in the whole of the kingdom.'

'But I like hunting,' complained the King. 'It's my favourite sport. It is the sport of kings – one of the things kings do.'

'Well, this particular king

had better stop doing it, or he'll have to stay in my cave for ever.'

At that moment the unicorn stuck her head round a rock. 'Please, Miss Rosie Dragon, is it safe? Can I have a peep at Mr King please?'

The King stared at the unicorn.

'A unicorn!' he cried. 'I never saw one before and she is so beautiful.'

'I know,' smiled the unicorn modestly. 'I am very beautiful indeed.'

'If you agree to let me have the unicorn,' cried the King, 'I promise to ban hunting in my realm. No king in the world has a unicorn. Is it a deal, Rosie?'

'Certainly not!' snapped the dragon, 'I don't own the unicorn. She can make up her own mind.'

'Please, please come back to Court with me. You can have fields to yourself and I would make no demands on you. I just want to be able to show people that I, King Pippin the Fourth, have a real, live beautiful unicorn at my Court. People would come from far and wide to see such an amazing sight. You would be treated as an honoured guest.'

'Oh!' said the unicorn. 'Well, that all sounds very nice, I will go with you Mr King, if that's all right with you, Miss Rosie Dragon.'

'Oh, suit yourself love, but only go if that's really what you want.'

'Well, I think I would be admired by a great many people. I would like that. I deserve it.'

'Oh, this is wonderful!' cried the King, 'And I shall call you Evangalina, a lovely name for a beautiful creature.'

'No,' said the unicorn, 'I'm sorry but I already have a name, Mr King. Miss Rosie Dragon threatened to turn me into a Crispy Noodle, and that is now my name.'

'Crispy Noodle!? You can't be serious. It's a horrible name!'

'Well, it's my name and I rather like it. So either you agree to call me Crispy Noodle or I won't come to Court with you.'

Reluctantly the King agreed.

'Well, that's all settled in a very satisfactory way,' commented Rosie. 'Come on, Kingy dear, on my back and I'll take you back to the castle. You come too, Crispy Noodle.'

As the procession passed through the forest the animals made a line along the path and bowed their heads as the King passed.

'They're saying "God Save

the King",' Rosie told him.

The King grinned from ear
to ear and waved to the animals
graciously.

'No more hunting!' he cried,
'You will all be safe here and

everywhere in my realm.'

Then he leaned over and whispered in Rosie's ear.

'More happy loyal subjects. Just as I like it to be.'

THE END

A SELECTED LIST OF TITLES AVAILABLE FROM YOUNG CORGI BOOKS

THE PRICES SHOWN BELOW WERE CORRECT AT THE TIME OF GOING TO PRESS. HOWEVER TRANSWORLD PUBLISHERS RESERVE THE RIGHT TO SHOW NEW RETAIL PRICES ON COVERS WHICH MAY DIFFER FROM THOSE PREVIOUSLY ADVERTISED IN THE TEXT OR ELSEWHERE.

☐ 52713 0	ROYAL BLUNDER	*Henrietta Branford*	£2.50
☐ 52524 3	GREEDY ALICE	*Helen Cresswell*	£1.75
☐ 52610 X	MAGNIFICENT MAX	*Terrance Dicks*	£2.50
☐ 52635 5	THE LITTLE DRAGON FALLS OUT	*Ann Jungman*	£2.50
☐ 52521 9	THE LITTLE DRAGON STEPS OUT	*Ann Jungman*	£2.25
☐ 52522 7	COUNT BORIS BOLESCU AND THE BLACK PUDDING	*Ann Jungman*	£2.25
☐ 52636 3	COUNT BORIS BOLESCU AND THE TRANSYLVANIAN TANGO	*Ann Jungman*	£2.50
☐ 52701 7	ROLAND AND THE GREEN KNIGHT	*Ann Jungman*	£2.50
☐ 52476 X	MIKE'S MAGIC SEEDS	*Alexander McCall Smith*	£2.50
☐ 52606 1	SUZY MAGICIAN	*Alexander McCall Smith*	£1.99
☐ 52445 X	DRAGON FIRE	*Ann Ruffell*	£1.99
☐ 52532 4	DRAGON WATER	*Ann Ruffell*	£1.75
☐ 52470 0	A PUFF OF SMOKE	*Catherine Sefton*	£1.99

All Young Corgi Books are available at your bookshop or newsagent, or can be ordered from the following address:

Transworld Publishers Ltd, Cash Sales Department,
PO Box 11, Falmouth, Cornwall TR10 9EN

Please send a cheque or postal order (no currency) and allow £1.00 for postage and packing for one book, an additional 50p for a second book, and an additional 30p for each subsequent book ordered to a maximum charge of £3.00 if ordering seven or more books.

Overseas customers, including Eire, please allow £2.00 for postage and packing for the first book, an additional £1.00 for a second book, and an additional 50p for each subsequent title ordered.

Name: ....

Address: ....

....